South and West Wales

Its Wildlife, People and Places

Marc Harris

Text copyright © Marc Harris 2022
Design copyright © Billie Hastie 2022
All rights reserved.

Marc Harris has asserted his right under the Copyright, Designs and Patents Act 1988 to be identified as the author of this work.

No part of this book may be reprinted or reproduced or utilised in any form or by electronic, mechanical or any other means, now known or hereafter invented, including photocopying or recording, or in any information storage or retrieval system, without the permission in writing from the Publisher and Author.

First published 2022
by Rowanvale Books Ltd
The Gate
Keppoch Street
Roath
Cardiff
CF24 3JW
www.rowanvalebooks.com

A CIP catalogue record for this book is available from the British Library.

Paperback ISBN: 978-1-913662-74-5
eBook ISBN: 978-1-913662-75-2

CONTENTS

Introduction   1

CARDIFF
The Beauty of Bute Park   3
The Peregrine Diaries   7
Sea Lamprey   11
A History of Hailey Park   15
In Memory of Mary Gillham, MBE.   19

THE VALE OF GLAMORGAN
The Hidden Gems of Barry Island   24
Walking the Welsh Jurassic Coast   29
Cosmeston Lakes Country Park   34
My Year in a Caravan (Trial by Fire and Ice)   39

CARMARTHENSHIRE
A Rural Retreat in Carmarthenshire   44
The National Botanic Gardens of Wales   52

INTRODUCTION

Bute Park in Autumn

The natural world has always been a real passion of mine. I have walked and cycled many thousands of miles in my life, often in pursuit of the 'wonders of nature', which has been the foundation of that unbridled passion.

This book will take you on a journey of discovery to many of the accessible, and sometimes more remote, locations you might find in south and west Wales. There are pieces on peregrine falcons in the clock tower of Cardiff's City Hall, the beauty of Bute Park, the National Botanic Gardens of Wales, and an account of the time I spent living on an isolated working sheep-farm in rural Carmarthenshire. Another account allows you to witness some of the hidden gems of Barry Island, and another takes you back into history, and prehistory, in *Walking the Welsh Jurassic Coast*.

Within these pages, you will encounter rare and unusual animals in the most surprising locations, such as the sea lamprey: a scarce and protected fish that has been present on our planet since before the age of the dinosaurs.

I have also documented the lives of people such as Mary Gillham MBE, a wonderful scientist and conservationist who is sadly no longer with us, but who deserves to be remembered for the conservation work she did, not only in Wales but around the world.

I grew up watching many of the wonderful natural history programmes of the 1970s, such as *The Undersea World of Jacques Cousteau* and *Survival*, and it was those programmes which inspired my interest in all aspects of the natural world, an unbridled fascination that has honed and shaped my thinking to this very day.

I hope you find something within these pages to interest, entertain and inspire you also.

Enjoy.

CARDIFF
THE BEAUTY OF BUTE PARK

Cardiff Castle

I had finished another night shift, just after the turn of the year, and was cycling my usual route home through Bute Park, in the centre of Cardiff. I had known Bute Park in all seasons, and even in the dark depths of a January morning, with the wind howling and the sun barely up, the arboretum had a kind of stark, spectral beauty.

In a few months, many of the trees, currently skeletal and devoid of leaves, would begin to flourish again. New growth would transform the park, and the flowerbeds, brown and bare in many places, would become a riot of colour.

The dark days of winter still held sway, but though the scent of spring was not yet in the air, the days were getting imperceptibly lighter and longer.

The history of the area goes back many centuries, and the activities of countless generations have moulded the landscape that is now Bute Park. Today's park is far removed from the site which initially attracted those people; the river and the castle being magnets for early settlements. Nowadays, the park is a public place, and a real green gem in the centre of the city. The park is also Grade-1 listed on Cadw's (Welsh Heritage) Register of Parks and Gardens of Special Historic Interest.

From about the 12th century, the land around the epicentres of the castle and river were used for religious purposes, cottage industries and agriculture. In 1766, the Bute family—wealthy landowners—inherited the castle, and from the 19th century onwards began to develop the site. The land around the castle was purchased and pleasurable gardens created.

The estate's development reflected the burgeoning prosperity and ambition that characterised Cardiff at the time, with architect William Burgess working alongside Andrew Pettigrew, the head gardener at Mount Stuart House, ancestral home of the Marquess of Bute, to create a landscape that augmented the intricate work on the castle.

In 1947, the fifth Marquess of Bute gifted both the castle and grounds to the people of Cardiff, and the land became a public park. Today the park is a jewel in the centre of the city, and a haven for wildlife. It is also a venue for many public events, including the annual visit of the RHS Flower Show.

Bute Park contains within its boundaries a nationally significant tree collection, an education centre, three cafés and myriad plants to interest the earnest horticulturalist.

The park itself covers an area of 56 hectares, which is equivalent to 75 football pitches. There are many things to do in the park, with several easy to navigate trails guiding you between them. Its landscape is a mixture of urban woodland, arboretum, sports pitches and historic vistas.

The area's history reflects the diverse development of Cardiff. There are many important heritage sites to visit, including Cardiff Castle, the Gorsedd Stones, the famous animal wall and the site of Blackfriars Friary.

The park's arboretum contains over three thousand individual tree species, which have been catalogued. The site has more 'champion trees' than any other UK public park, which gives the area great prestige, champion trees being the tallest and broadest examples of their species found anywhere in Great Britain.

Indeed, there is so much to do and to see in this green space, and I have seen some wonderful sights over the years.

Cycling has always been a great passion of mine, and I have cycled through the park on many occasions, in all seasons. I have watched the blue flash of kingfishers as they dart along the Dock Feeder Stream, and have fished that very same stream, catching small fish such as dace, roach, chub and grayling, all of which are an absolute delight to play on a small fly rod. And, of course, being environmentally conscious as I am, I have always made sure the fish are returned to the water in a healthy state.

I have regularly watched the activities of dippers and wagtails as they bob up and down on the bank in their differing ways and, even, on a couple of occasions, witnessed the exceedingly rare site of the spawning sequence of sea lamprey—a rare and endangered fish which has been present on our planet since before the dinosaurs.

Over the years, I have also watched peregrine falcons and buzzards flying high over the area. Bute Park is also notable as a breeding ground of the scarce lesser spotted woodpecker, a sparrow-sized woodpecker I have observed on occasion clinging to tree-trunks, high in the tree canopy.

Otters have also been seen in the park, but I must admit, I have not yet been lucky enough to see one.

Yes, Bute Park is a wonderful place, and a real green gem in the heart of Cardiff. Please come and visit if you can. I know you will not be disappointed.

Bute Park is open 365 days a year. It is easily accessible from Cardiff Central Station.

There are also regular bus stops close to the park. Pay and display car parking facilities are available nearby in Sophia Gardens.

A Waterbus also operates on the River Taff, carrying passengers to and from Cardiff Bay.

THE PEREGRINE DIARIES

I first became involved with the RSPB as a volunteer after the dramatic rescue of a peregrine falcon chick on the lawns in front of Cardiff's Civic Centre, in 2008.

I was working on the Night-Bus: a refurbished double-decker which served teas, coffees and sandwiches to homeless people on the streets. It was a warm, dry June evening and my first shift on the bus, which was parked outside the steps of the National Museum of Wales.

At approximately 8:30 p.m., as the homeless people began to disperse for the night, I noticed a commotion on the grass some distance away. A young woman, who we later discovered to be a zoology student, was chasing a large bird across the lawns in front of the bus, trying her best to throw her cardigan over it. The bird had been hit by a car. Being an enthusiastic, if somewhat amateur ornithologist, I presumed the creature to be one of the gulls that wheeled and soared in the city's skies throughout the day.

When the bird, which was being mobbed by several gulls, was finally caught, we telephoned the RSPCA and waited for rescue.

The bird—which turned out to be a peregrine chick—was wrapped in the cardigan, and a homeless person took charge, cradling it in one arm 'like a babe in swaddling clothes'. From time to time, we checked on its progress, making sure the needle-sharp beak and talons were kept far away from human flesh. Its dark, liquid eyes seemed to transfix us all. The peregrine remained remarkably calm throughout its ordeal.

At 10 p.m., an RSPCA van arrived, with a film crew from the television programme *Animal Rescue 24/7*. As filming continued, the peregrine was duly examined and placed in a cage for transportation.

A few days later, I was really pleased to learn that the chick, a female, was unharmed. It was ringed for identification purposes and would soon be released from the top of City Hall, close to where its parents were nesting.

The chicks had hatched in early May as tiny balls of fluff. Their parents had commandeered an old ravens' nest, just above the City Hall clock, which faced south towards Cardiff Bay. They had chased the unfortunate ravens away.

Three eggs were laid, and the three chicks seemed to be doing well.

To me, there were a few stars of the show: the zoologist who initially caught the chick, the homeless people who cared for it so tenderly and, of course, the peregrine herself.

A week later, I contacted the RSPB at their headquarters in Sutherland House in Cardiff and volunteered for the 'Aren't Birds Brilliant!' project, since renamed 'A Date with Nature', which was being run in conjunction with the National Museum of Wales. Volunteering involved showing people the peregrines of City Hall clock tower and promoting the principles of the RSPB.

After some paperwork was completed, confirming my newfound status as a volunteer, my first shift at the museum began in early July. Immediately, it became obvious that the public's fascination for these birds knew no bounds. Indeed, some people could scarcely believe that peregrine falcons were nesting in a city.

Personally, I likened the tower to an urban clifftop, with a plentiful supply of food. In rural areas, cliffs would be the peregrines' natural home, and wild wood pigeons or rock doves their natural food. They had just moved into the city and found a perfect nesting site, and a perfect supply of prey.

The RSPB had a small stand inside the museum from which the birds could be viewed on a webcam. We handed out leaflets, gave out information about the peregrines and signed up new members. We helped people see the peregrines through telescopes and binoculars from various vantage points outside.

There were some great views of the adults and chicks, and people were often in awe of the birds. In good weather, we'd assemble a marquee on the lawns in front of the museum. Sometimes the chicks could be heard calling for food—a shrill, eerie, piercing cry—and the parents would regularly return with a kill.

On one occasion, I watched the female chick through a telescope. When fully grown, the female is a third bigger than the male, enabling her to hunt larger prey, thereby supplying a variety of food to the youngsters throughout the breeding season. I marvelled as she hopped and flapped above a ledge, playing with what looked like a pigeon carcass. It was almost comical to watch as she moved the body along the ledge for more than half an hour. It was wonderful to see that she was doing well.

The peregrine is a formidable hunter, and its dive, or stoop as it is known, has been timed at over two hundred miles per hour, making it the fastest bird in the world. This, along with the predatory, almost regal appearance of the birds, had clearly endeared them to the public.

In other cities, pigeons are said to comprise more than forty percent of the peregrines' diet, and although songbirds and waders are also predated upon, we had occasional reports of our adult peregrines attacking and killing gulls.

As the project came to a close, towards the end of August, both adults and the three chicks were assumed to still be alive, although they were rarely seen together. As their nest of sticks began to disintegrate, I wondered where the birds, particularly the juveniles, might go. The name peregrine derives from the Latin for 'wanderer', and as the birds in the wild can live up to 17 years, it was anybody's guess where they might end up. If the chicks did not leave the nest of their own accord, it was inevitable that the adults would drive them away as they competed for food.

The peregrine family had become so popular; thousands of people had enjoyed watching them over the summer. In fact, they had become a real tourist attraction. My only hope was that the adults would return next spring to produce another clutch of peregrine eggs.

I guessed the public would miss the peregrines.

I knew I would.

The birds returned to nest on the clock tower for the next two years. In 2009, no chicks were born. In 2010, as I write this article, we are hopeful that the adults will produce young.

As of 2021, I believe the peregrines still nest on the clock tower to this very day and have produced several offspring over the years since I last volunteered for the RSPB.

N.B. A tiercel is the name given to a male peregrine falcon. Tiercel is derived from the French, meaning third. The male peregrine is a third smaller than the female, which is called a falcon.

SEA LAMPREY

The sun was shining on a warm June day in 2011. I had worked up a sweat cycling some ten miles in total along the Taff Trail, part of the national cycle network, which leads north from the centre of Cardiff and ends some 55 miles later in the town of Brecon. The trail itself runs near the River Taff for several miles.

I had seen nothing remarkable as I cycled, although otters, salmon and sea trout had now returned to a river 'that once ran black with coal dust'—a legacy of the dark days of the mining industry in Wales. Indeed, I regularly watched kingfishers, dippers and various coarse and game fish, including barbel, which had been introduced to the water some twenty years before and were now being caught at weights over sixteen pounds within sight of the Millennium Stadium (now renamed the Principality Stadium).

That day, however, my rather unremarkable cycle ride was suddenly to become quite special. I had stopped for a rest by the bridge at Blackweir, a mile from the city centre, just at the point where the Dock Feeder Stream flows out of the Taff and into the magnificent arboretum of Bute Park. As I looked down into the shallow, fast-flowing waters of the stream, I was amazed to see a pair of sea lamprey spawning. Having seen pictures of these eel-like creatures before, I knew that they were, without doubt, sea lamprey. The male, which was approximately four feet long, was engrossed in a mating ritual with a female about half his size. A redd had been dug, and he was gripping relatively large stones with his bony, suckered mouth, then moving them some distance away from the depression in the gravel the couple's love dance had created. I marvelled at the colours of their mottled backs as the pair continued their sinuous, sensual embrace.

I was transfixed. Here, within a stone's throw of the city centre of Cardiff, I was witnessing the mating ritual of a fish that fossil evidence has shown predates the dinosaurs. A fish with no scales, gill covers, or bony skeleton. A fish that is now an endangered species and protected by law.

To my right, on the far bank of the river, were the sports grounds of Cooper's Field, where hundreds of students from the local universities had gathered. Many were enjoying barbecues as they frolicked and lounged in the hot summer sun, all apparently in blissful ignorance of the prehistoric creatures just a short distance away.

But back to the Feeder Stream, and something about the incredible life cycle of the sea lamprey.

The sea lamprey, or *Petromyzon marinus*, to give it its Latin name, is a parasitic fish. It uses its suction-cup-like mouth to attach itself to a wide variety of other fish and rasp away flesh with its probing tongue and teeth. Anticoagulants in the lamprey's mouth prevent the victim's blood from clotting, and those victims often die from loss of blood, or infection. Young lampreys, or ammocoetes, lie buried in the soft, silty beds of river margins. They are blind and feed on tiny particles in the water. After several years as larvae, they metamorphose into adults and migrate to sea estuaries where they parasitise other fish, returning to spawn in spring or early summer, usually on the stony ground of gravel beds. The adults do not feed after spawning and die within a few days.

And that latter stage in the sea lamprey's lifecycle, the spawning stage—the final act of the courting couple—was the scene that unfolded before my very eyes.

After about half an hour, I cycled home, leaving the lampreys to their own devices. I had taken some photographs, and sent them into the Environment Agency, now named Natural Resources Wales. Although my pictures were not great—they were taken from the bridge with a compact camera—the Environment Agency were incredibly pleased to hear from me and confirmed my sightings as rare sea lamprey.

Some days later, I returned to the same spot, and in the margins of the Dock Feeder Stream, anchored amongst some stones, I saw what appeared to be the decomposing remains of a fish. Much of the body had already been eaten, so it was difficult to tell precisely what species it might have been. Whether it was the remains of a sea lamprey or not, I was glad I had witnessed the spawning sequence of the living fish. Fish that were around before the dinosaurs. Scarce fish that had returned to the ecosystem of the river in small numbers, to an ecosystem that at one time was so polluted.

In June 2015, I once again spotted some sea lamprey spawning in the Dock Feeder Stream. On three separate days at the end of June in that year, and in precisely the same location as my sightings in 2011, I observed the fish again. This time, however, I saw as many as six of the prehistoric creatures in one day and counted eleven fish in total. I reported my sightings to

Natural Resources Wales, who passed them on to their records department.

In the seventeen years I have been cycling along the Taff Trail, it is only twice I have witnessed sea lamprey spawning. I count myself incredibly lucky that I have witnessed such a rare sight.

Since 2015, I have looked, every year, in the month of June, for these rare and protected fish in the Dock Feeder Stream.

I have not seen a sea lamprey since.

For nearly eight hundred years, the good people of Gloucester have sent our reigning monarch a decorated lamprey pie to mark jubilees and coronations. The fish were caught in the River Severn. During the industrial revolution, as tastes changed, the practice died out, but was revived in 1953 by Howard Sibson, then Gloucester's sheriff.

For the Queen's Diamond Jubilee, because of the scarcity and protected status of sea lampreys in Britain, the fish had to be imported from the Great Lakes in Canada. In May 2012, a representative of The Great Lakes Fisheries Commission presented lampreys to the city council, to enable the traditional pie to be baked.

Of course, it is well known that Henry I died from eating a "surfeit of lampreys;" so, if the Queen does partake of this ancient delicacy, perhaps the consumption of just a small morsel would be wise.

It is not known to this day whether Her Majesty has ever tasted one of the pies.

A HISTORY OF HAILEY PARK

A Peacock Butterfly

Hailey Park, formerly a landfill site, now managed by a team of rangers from Cardiff Council's Parks Department in conjunction with volunteers, has become a haven for wildlife.

The park, some four miles north of Cardiff, through which the Taff Trail passes, has been designated a Site of Importance for Nature Conservation since 2009. Within the park's boundaries are a myriad of habitats including a beautiful wildflower meadow and a woodland that is both thinned and coppiced, allowing light to reach the ground, encouraging flowers such as celandines, wood anemones and bluebells to flourish in season.

In 2007, a group of park users and local residents formed the Friends of Hailey Park, an organisation which now numbers over 100, dedicated to improving the area for both wildlife and park users alike. The Friends of Hailey Park were awarded a Green Flag Community Award in 2013 for their meadow management work. The volunteers work closely with the rangers from the Parks Department, police, schools, Friends of the Earth and Sustrans, carrying out maintenance in the area to encourage regeneration of the meadow and increase biodiversity. Paths are maintained, regular litter picks carried out, and the scrub cut back, which if left untouched would return the park to a tangle of willow, brambles and buddleia. They also organise regular wildlife walks, which seem quite popular.

To become a Friend of Hailey Park is not expensive, only £3 per annum, and with more members, more voluntary work can be carried out and further grant funding applied for. Volunteers are asked to wear suitable clothing when carrying out activities, and children are actively encouraged, although they must be supervised by an adult. All tools are provided.

The park, which holds a central position in the River Taff Valley, also has fantastic views up the valley itself. Recent grant funding and planting has made the area extremely popular with dog walkers and cyclists alike. Users of the park are asked to respect each other's space, and in general, this seems to happen.

In summer, the managed scrub becomes a riot of colour, attracting all sorts of insects to the rich nectar of the wildflower meadow. Purple hairstreak and brown hairstreak butterflies are sometimes seen in the park, although the former are more likely to be glimpsed fleetingly at the top of oak trees, where they like to fly.

I myself have spent many years wandering around Hailey Park in all seasons. The park is a joy to behold at any time, but as a member of Butterfly Conservation, I especially enjoy the summer months when the wildflowers are at their best and butterflies can be observed from close quarters without too much disturbance. In recent years, I've participated in the Big Butterfly Count, which simply involves sitting or standing quietly in an area, which can be your own garden, and counting the different species of butterfly which appear in any given 15-minute period, then recording and reporting those sightings to Butterfly Conservation. It is not at all difficult and is a great way to monitor species diversity in an area. For Butterfly Conservation, it is also a great way to check the health of butterflies and map the increase or decrease of butterfly species across the United Kingdom.

Butterflies such as the peacock, gatekeeper, small white, common blue and meadow brown are all seen regularly in Hailey Park. Small tortoiseshells are also seen, although I believe there has been a dramatic decline in the sightings of this insect, not just in the park, but nationally, since I was a child.

In the summer of 2014, I counted over 10 different species of butterfly in one golden 15-minute period. I spotted nothing rare as I soaked up the sun, although one significant sighting was the Essex skipper. This butterfly had been first discovered in Hailey Park relatively recently by one of the rangers, which was the first time the butterfly had ever been seen in Glamorgan.

On one rather special occasion, some years ago, I had one of my best sightings as a clouded yellow alighted on a buddleia only a few feet away from me. It was a fantastic sight to see an insect rarely seen in the park at such close quarters. In October, I have also watched hornets, hovering like miniature helicopters, supping nectar from those same buddleia flowers. And on late spring days, encountered tangles of slow worms, seeking warmth from beneath strategically placed sheets of corrugated iron. On another occasion, I watched with incredulity as the biggest grass snake I have ever seen swam sinuously across the river to hunt amongst the rocks and boulders on the far bank. It would be no exaggeration to say that the grass snake was at least four feet long.

Over the Taff itself, I have regularly watched the activities of dippers and kingfishers as they have hunted for prey, and although I have yet to see an otter, I know they are there.

Yes, Hailey Park is a wonderful place, and one of my favourite places to visit and observe wildlife. It is a place I hope to visit for many years to come, which in part is thanks to the council, rangers and volunteers who have made it the incredibly special place it is today. A haven for wildlife, and a mecca for biodiversity.

A Tangle of Slow Worms

IN MEMORY OF MARY GILLHAM, MBE.

Mary Gillham
Image courtesy of *Dr Mary Gillham/Mary Gillham Archive Project (SEWBRec)*.

I feel a strong affinity with Mary Gillham. I have spent many years cycling and walking the Taff Trail—a Sustrans cycle route which stretches from Cardiff to Brecon—observing, recording and writing about the wildlife of the area.

Indeed, I have cycled the whole route itself, some years ago, but have also spent many happy hours in the last 16 years exploring 'my local patch': Forest Farm Country Park, which Mary, as a naturalist and writer herself, knew so well.

The Hide in the Memorial Fields

Forest Farm Country Park lies approximately five miles north of Cardiff and is only a short distance from where I used to live in the city centre. The country park encompasses a designated nature reserve and a Site of Special Scientific Interest (Glamorgan Canal and Long Wood). Long Wood is a semi-natural ancient woodland, and the designated nature reserve contains a variety of habitats, which include wetlands, open water, and semi-improved grassland. Two bird hides overlook the wetlands, and an artificial sand martin cliff has been built in one of the hides. I have personally observed birds as diverse as water rail and snipe, and bittern have also been seen in recent years. A heronry has also become established on a nearby site, and if you walk along the canal on any warm, sunny day, you will encounter all sorts of insect and aquatic life.

But now, a bit more about Mary Gillham.

Dr Mary Gillham MBE dedicated herself to wildlife and was the founding member of the Glamorgan Naturalists' Trust and the Cardiff Naturalists' Society. She gained a degree in agriculture, and first-class honours in botany and completed a PhD on Skokholm Island.

As one of the highlights of a truly memorable career, she was one of the first women to join an Antarctic expedition in 1959. She was also involved in saving a remote coral island from destruction due to development, thus preserving its rare and exotic wildlife for posterity. She lectured all over the world in universities as far apart as New Zealand, Australia, Nigeria and England, and worked in the Adult Education Department of University College Cardiff until her retirement in 1988. In her younger days, Mary also hitch-hiked her way across South Africa and visited the Americas and Africa and islands in the Indian Ocean, where she led groups of naturalists and was involved in many research projects. In World War Two she volunteered for the Women's Land Army.

Although I have considerable admiration for Mary's many exploits around the world, and have even travelled and explored some of the more remote areas of Europe myself, including the French and Spanish Pyrenees, it was really our mutual love of the ecology of south-east Wales—and in particular, this corner of south-east Wales, Forest Farm Country Park, where both she and I spent so many hours observing the local wildlife on 'our local patch'—which drew me to her.

A recently converted barn, close to the warden's centre, in the country park, has been turned into a hide. The hide now overlooks two ponds and a small orchard, which attracts all manner of wildlife including grass snakes, slow worms and many species of birds and insects. It really is a beautiful spot and has quite rightly been named in honour of Mary Gillham, being designated 'The Mary Gillham Memorial Fields'. A quote inside the hide, alluding to Mary herself, "Inspiring the next generation of naturalists", seems to define her in a nutshell.

A Female Bullfinch   A Male Bullfinch

Nearby, an 18th-century farmhouse has been converted into a conservation centre for the site, which is also now home to the British Trust for Conservation Volunteers (BCTV). The warden's centre also serves as a base for the Cardiff Council Countryside Wardens Team and is used as an educational environmental resource to nurture an interest and healthy regard for nature amongst schools and special interest groups. The former tree nursery is now a woodland recycling centre, converting fallen or storm-damaged trees into wood chip and park furniture.

Dr Mary Gillham MBE died on the 24th of March 2013, aged 91. She was awarded the MBE for services to nature conservation in South Wales in 2008. Perhaps it was fitting that her last home was nearby at Radyr, not far from Forest Farm Country Park, close to the area she knew so well. She very reluctantly had to sell her beloved cottage at the base of Garth Mountain, Gwaelod y Garth, where she had lived for many years, and move to a flat, as she finally admitted that even for such an active person, she was slowing down.

And yes, she is still "inspiring the next generation of naturalists".

Although I never met Mary, I'd like to think I am one of those naturalists.

If you can, just take a moment to sit in the hide overlooking the Mary Gillham Memorial Fields; it is truly a beautiful place. Or if you cannot do that, maybe seek out and read one of her many books. Mary wrote so eloquently and passionately about so many aspects of the natural world.

She is a lady who deserves to be remembered.

RECOMMENDED READING

Seabirds. (Instructions to Young Ornithologists IV), Museum Press: London, 1963.

A Naturalist in New Zealand, Museum Press: London, 1966.

Sub-Antarctic Sanctuary: Summertime on Macquarie Island, Victor Gollancz: London, 1967.

Town Bred, Country Nurtured: A Naturalist Looks Back Fifty Years, independently published, 1998.

Islands of the Trade Winds: An Indian Ocean Odyssey, Minerva Press: London, 2000.

A Natural History of Cardiff, Dinefwr Publishers ltd: Wales, 2004.

Wildlife Watching in the Slow Lane, Halsgrove, 2009. This was her last published book.

THE VALE OF GLAMORGAN
THE HIDDEN GEMS OF BARRY ISLAND

Jackson's Bay

When you think of Barry Island, I am sure your first thoughts are of funfairs, amusement arcades and overcrowded, sandy beaches. But if you look closely, behind this facade, you will soon discover some wonderful walks, a fascinating history and some real treasures of the natural world.

Barry Island, named after the 6th-century Saint Baruc, forms part of the town of Barry in the Vale of Glamorgan. What is now a peninsula was in fact an island until the 1880s, when it was linked to the mainland as the town of Barry increased in size. This, in part, was due to the opening of Barry Dock by the Barry Dock Railway Company. Barry's stretch of coastline on the Bristol Channel has the world's second highest tidal range of 15 metres, or 49 feet, second only to that of the Bay of Fundy in eastern Canada. That tidal range, as an occasional angler, is something of which I am acutely aware.

In July 2015, my friend and I caught a train from Cardiff with the intention of fishing from the rocks at Barry Island. Although it was a warm, sunny day, fishing with light tackle, as we'd intended, proved impossible as the wind whipped the waves into white horses and hurled them against the rocks. With little weight on our lines, we were simply unable to cast into that gale. Still, if we could not fish, we could always walk, and as both my friend and I were interested in all aspects of the natural world, we thought we would start by walking the concrete path above the beach at Barry Island (Whitmore Bay), in the direction of Jackson's Bay. Jackson's Bay, with its golden sands, secluded nature and pleasant views, must surely be one of Barry's best kept secrets.

As we walked, we discussed the six-foot-long swordfish that had been found washed up on Whitmore Bay in 2008, and although we had no expectation of finding such a rarity, we hoped we might discover other unusual animals or plants. We were both members of Butterfly Conservation and were always on the lookout for an unusual butterfly or moth. We were keenly aware there was always the possibility of the sighting of a migrant hummingbird hawkmoth or a clouded yellow.

Suffice to say that we saw neither of these majestic insects, but we did discover several colonies of small blues, Britain's smallest butterfly and now something of a relative rarity. I marvelled at the tenacity of these tiny insects, whose forewings were almost black, or dark brown, with a dusting of blue, as they flitted from flower to flower, barely flying more than a foot above the sparse coastal vegetation, which is their shield and sanctuary from the powerful winds that blow off the sea. To me, for such tiny butterflies, their struggle for survival in such adverse weather conditions borders on the truly heroic!

Below the coastal lookout station at Nell's Point, natural springs above the cliffs have worn away holes in the softer rocks below and pools of freshwater have gathered at the cliff base. As we continued to walk the concrete footpath, above us, from the tangle of foliage which strangles the cliff face, came the clap of a wood pigeon's wings, accompanied by the melodious voice of a song thrush.

Looking out to sea, in the direction of North Devon, the islands of Flat Holm and Steep Holm dominate the Bristol Channel. Several years previously, I had spent a long adventure weekend on Flat Holm. It is well worth a visit, with some unique flora and fauna, and a history that goes back thousands of years. The island can be accessed from Cardiff or Weston-Super-Mare via a daily boat trip, and visitors can spend up to six hours on Flat Holm enjoying a wonderful day out.

In the foliage at the base of the cliffs, I spotted a nest (tent) that was once home to a species of caterpillar. The web-like structure had long since been vacated, but the tent had survived the worst the elements could throw at it and so, hopefully, had most of the caterpillars.

As we approached the seclusion of Jackson's Bay, I spotted the distinctive purple flowers of deadly nightshade, or belladonna as it is also known, sheltering amongst the other plants at the base of the cliff. The plant, a member of the tomato family, is highly toxic to humans, so must not be touched under any circumstances. The consumption of just a small number of berries can prove fatal. Nevertheless, it was very interesting to observe such a plant so toxic to us but important for wildlife in its natural environment. Despite the toxicity of the berries, animals do eat them, finding them sweet, and disperse the seeds of the plant in their droppings.

As my friend and I came to the end of our walk, and we clambered down onto the golden sands of Jackson's Bay, we had almost forgotten about fishing. Despite the wind, we had really enjoyed our short journey, which had taken us barely a mile from the funfairs and amusement arcades so often associated with Barry Island. Yes, Barry Island has far more to offer than the superficial; there are some wonderful animals, plants and secret places to discover.

Take my advice and look beyond the hustle and bustle. You never know what you might find.

POSTSCRIPT

If you were to take a different route, and travel in the opposite direction from Whitmore Bay, I would recommend walking to the headland at Friar's Point. The headland is one of the best examples of calcareous, cowslip-dominated hay meadow in south-east Wales, and is an area of Special Scientific Interest. It is home to a variety of butterflies, bees, grasshoppers and other insects, and it is a location where I have spotted another relative insect rarity: the grizzled skipper—a small, pretty, almost speckled butterfly which is sadly struggling to survive in many of its old habitats across Britain. Its presence there amongst the wildflowers on the grassy headland was a most welcome sight.

The headland is also home to a medieval pillow mound where rabbits were kept in medieval times and bred as an important food source. And if you continue onwards, walking to the end of the track, before turning right, you will come across the old harbour, with its share of rusting and rotting hulks and a history going back centuries.

But perhaps that history is for another day.

A Decaying Hulk in the Old Harbour

WALKING THE WELSH JURASSIC COAST

The Welsh Jurassic Coast

It was a warm, sunny day in the middle of May when I began my walk on the Welsh Coastal Path on the cliffs at Penarth, in the direction of St Mary's Well Bay. It was a journey that would take me back, not only into history, but into prehistory itself. In the space of a few miles, I would encounter the building known as Marconi Tower, the abandoned ruins of Lavernock Fort, and an area on the beach where the fossilised skeleton of the first meat-eating dinosaur to be found in Wales was recently discovered.

The walk was clearly signposted, and although a thick tangle of hedgerow obscured the sea view and the precipitous cliffs, there were occasional gaps where I could gaze out to sea. The path was relatively flat with only a few slight inclines to contend with, so walking was not at all difficult. Inland, arable fields stretched for some distance, whilst alongside the path, delicate butterflies such as orange tip, speckled wood and green-veined whites flitted amongst the abundant fragrant wildflowers. In the spring sunshine, blackbirds and the occasional thrush sang melodiously from deep in the tangle of hawthorn, whilst in the azure-blue skies above, gulls wheeled and soared on thermals.

At one point, the path dropped to beach level and rose again, and it was then that I came across a small and rather innocuous ivy-covered building on the clifftop—Marconi Tower. It was there that in 1897 the first wireless signals were exchanged between Lavernock Point and Flat Holm Island. Not far from the hut, and standing on the cliff edge, was a Royal Observation Corps observation post. During the war, volunteer ROC observers spotted many German planes approaching from across the channel and activated air raid warnings in nearby Penarth. In early 1962, a nuclear bunker was completed at Lavernock Point for the ROC, with instruments to detect nuclear explosions and warn the public of fallout, but this was closed and abandoned in 1975 after repeated break-ins by vandals.

Marconi's transmitted messages were a momentous event in history, and a plaque inscribed in a perimeter wall of the nearby St Lawrence Church commemorates that moment. The first ever message transmitted in Morse code read, 'Are you ready?' followed by, 'Can you hear me?' The reply received was, 'Yes loud and clear.' The Morse code recording slip for this first message is

Saint Lawrence Church

now kept in the National Museum of Wales. St Lawrence Church itself, constructed mainly of limestone, is believed to date back to 1769 and although it rarely opens now, has a beautifully tended graveyard which is a haven for wildlife.

My walk then took a slight detour inland, where I found Marconi Holiday Park. At the back of the holiday park, you will find Lavernock Point Nature Reserve, which is a delight to behold. The nature reserve contains a wide variety of habitats, including Jurassic limestone grass and scrub. It is an important location for migrating birds and is also known for its hay meadows where orchids, cowslips and the scarce Adder's-tongue Fern can be seen in season. The elusive purple hairstreak butterfly can also be spotted from time to time at Oak Copse, which is north of Fort Road.

Soon after passing the nature reserve, I came across the ruins of Lavernock Fort. This site has an exceedingly long history dating back to the 1860s, when the Royal Commission built the gun battery to protect the channel approaches to Cardiff and Bristol's shipyards during the short-lived conflict between France and Britain that followed the French Revolution. Before 1895, a fourth cannon was added to the gun battery, and in 1903 all four guns were replaced by two rapid-fire six-inch ex-naval guns. In the Second World War, a searchlight battery was added, giving protection to shipping convoys between Cardiff, Barry and Flat Holm Island. Nowadays, the main section of the gun battery has been listed as an ancient monument, which includes the gun emplacements, crew and officers' quarters, and rangefinder observation position.

I had been walking for a couple of hours, and as I approached St Mary's Well Bay, I decided to sit down on the grass to eat my lunch. It was a great place to take a break. Below me, at the base of the cliffs, in the quiet swell, the waves washed lazily against the rocks.

It was mid-afternoon as I retraced my steps along the coastal path in the direction of Penarth. As I clambered down to the beach at Lavernock, I wondered what secrets the beach might hold, for in March 2014, two brothers and keen fossil hunters came across the discovery of a lifetime: the fossilised skeleton of a completely new species of dinosaur. The bones turned out to belong to the first meat-eating dinosaur to be found in Wales and a cousin of Tyrannosaurus rex. They were approximately 200 million years old, from a time when the Welsh climate was akin to that of the Mediterranean, with warm and shallow seas. The dinosaur would have stood less than three feet tall, was carnivorous and warm-blooded, and was probably covered in feathery down and quills along its back. It walked upright on two legs and had a long tail. It had apparently died when it was young, close to the shoreline, and was fossilised in marine sediment along with other small sea creatures.

As I climbed back onto the coastal path and neared the end of my walk at Penarth, I reflected on what a great day I'd had. I would recommend the walk to anyone. Whether you are a fan of nature, history, or prehistory, the Welsh Jurassic Coast is a brilliant place to explore. The walk is not difficult; try it for yourself.

Who knows what you might discover?

COSMESTON LAKES COUNTRY PARK

One of the Lakes at Cosmeston

I now live less than a quarter of a mile from Cosmeston Lakes Country Park, yet it is a place I have been coming to for a long time.

The park has, over the years, had several uses. It has been a limestone quarry, and even a tip for household waste. The area has since been reclaimed for the benefit of local people and, of course, wildlife, which flourishes in this carefully managed environment.

A number of lakes, formed after quarrying ended in the 1970s, are a haven for all manner of waterfowl. These lakes filled naturally with water because of the high-water table, forming the features you see today.

Within the park's boundaries are several distinctive habitats designed to encourage nature. There are meadows, woodlands, marshy areas and scrubland, a dragonfly pond and even a conservation area to which no access is allowed. An audio nature trail, available in both English and Welsh, gives information at certain locations about the history and wildlife you might discover in the park. There is also a visitor centre and a café, which are both well used.

Designated walks have their routes mapped out, ranging between one and three miles in length, and are graded as easy, medium and advanced, so that anyone walking in the park can choose a defined route, appropriate to their abilities.

During the 1970s, when the park was being constructed, the remains of a medieval village were discovered on the site. The village has since been rebuilt, with each building now standing where it originally stood, providing visitors with a unique insight into an Anglo-Welsh community in the 14th century. During the archaeological excavation, artefacts were found dating back to the time of Edward I, and Roman Samian pottery was also discovered. The village is well worth a visit, as wherever possible, buildings such as the Peasant's Cottage, Baker's House and Tithe Barn are used for their original purpose.

My own experiences of the park were enhanced immeasurably when I became an RSPB volunteer approximately ten years ago. I had previously volunteered in Cardiff, assisting with the project monitoring the peregrine falcons in the City Hall clock tower. Although I had very much enjoyed that experience, the project based in the foyer of the café in Cosmeston Country

Park provided me with a new challenge in a different environment.

I worked alongside an employee of the RSPB, and we signed up members, provided information about the birds and wildlife in the area, and recommended locations where not only common, but rare and unusual birds might be found.

An absolute highlight for me was the regular sighting of a bearded tit in the reed beds not far from the café. This is a small, beautifully marked bird with a long tail. It is a Schedule 1 listed bird with a blue head and a brown body. The male of the species, which is the bird that was regularly sighted, sported a striking black moustache, not a beard, and although the female is just as attractive, she lacks this distinctive feature.

There are approximately only 600 breeding pairs in Britain, and this normally scarce, shy and elusive bird made regular appearances in the reeds along the boardwalk, delighting passers-by.

In more recent times, I have seen foxes and watched a young stoat skip and frolic in the hedgerow on a bright summer's day. Not far from the park's boundaries, I have watched kestrels, woodpeckers, red kites and sparrowhawks and have regularly sighted buzzards soaring above the scrubland in their search for prey. In autumn, I have even rescued baby hedgehogs from the nearby road, carrying them to safety and placing them in the hedge and pointing their noses in the direction of the woods in the hope that they will be safe!

On one particular autumn night, at about 9 p.m., I was cycling through the park to begin a night shift in Cardiff. The park was completely deserted at this time—the dog walkers, horse riders and families having long since sought the sanctuary of their homes. It was then that I heard a faint rustling in the hedge to my right. In an instant, a tawny owl—a bird you can regularly hear calling in the area but rarely see—took off from its perch, arcing its way no more than a few feet above my head. I had a fleeting glimpse of a haunting, silent silhouette as it vanished into the clear night sky.

It was a wonderful sight to witness, of a bird that is relatively common but so seldom seen. In fact, I had not seen a tawny owl for 15 years, and I had completely forgotten just how big they are. An owl with a one metre wingspan, flying a few feet above your head, against the backdrop of a cloudless, starry night sky is surely a sight to be treasured.

In the autumn of 2019, I paid a visit to the visitor centre, and asked if any rare animals or birds had been sighted recently. The receptionist told me there were regular releases of water voles in the reeds along the boardwalks, not far from the café, and the last release of these wonderful little animals had taken place in October of that year. The decline of this mammal—in part due to the proliferation of mink, which has decimated populations across the United Kingdom—has been well documented, so it was great to see true conservation in action. I was subsequently told the water voles are now breeding on site, and this really made my day!

The lakes are also home to many species of fish, including pike, eels, carp, roach and rudd. I have often observed carp, perhaps weighing as much as 20 pounds, basking in the summer sunshine in the lake margins where the water is relatively shallow.

Although the lakes often appear tranquil, they can be a dangerous place for swimmers. Being an old quarry, there are many hidden snags under the water's surface—the bottom of the quarry is littered with abandoned machinery including cranes and bulldozers that were left behind as the quarry flooded—and it can be deceptively cold in summer. There are signs everywhere warning people not to swim, as there have been several fatalities over the years, yet people still choose to risk their lives in the summer months when the weather is inevitably warmer.

A cautionary tale perhaps, but a friend of my mother's was once married to a man who used to be a commercial diver. He used to practise diving in the lakes, as this was good training for his job. One day, as he was approaching the surface, he felt something grab and tug at one of his feet. On the surface, it was only when his wife pulled off his wetsuit and flippers that she noticed the two clear puncture wounds in his foot. Other divers I have known have confirmed that there are exceptionally large eels and pike in the lake, so maybe he had been grabbed by one of these leviathans from the murky depths. The Cosmeston Lakes Monster, perhaps? Who knows? But having discussed this story with the actual diver's wife, I have no doubts about the veracity of the tale in question!

Yet, despite all this, I can assure you that Cosmeston Lakes Country Park is well worth a visit. It is a fascinating and captivating place, and a haven for wildlife.

If you can, try and experience the park for yourself. I know you will not be disappointed.

MY YEAR IN A CARAVAN
(TRIAL BY FIRE AND ICE)

The Author's Caravan during The Beast from the East

In 2018, I moved to live in my caravan, at least for ten months of the year, to a site at St Mary's Well Bay, in the Vale of Glamorgan. It is a very picturesque site, with a nature reserve, woodlands, a coastline steeped in history, and a beach famous for its fossils nearby.

With stunning views of the Bristol Channel, punctuated by the islands of Flat Holm and Steep Holm, the site has much to offer. Western-Super-Mare is visible to the naked eye on a clear day, but a good pair of binoculars can enhance spectacular views. All manner of ships negotiate the channel, which can be very treacherous due to its great tidal range and powerful currents. From the window of my caravan, I watched, in all weathers, ships ranging from huge tankers and ferries to tiny yachts and fishing boats crossing the sea.

I moved to my caravan from the city of Cardiff, where I was born, simply for peace of mind. After 25 years in two separate spells in the Welsh capital, I had just had enough of city life. And, of course, as an inveterate nature lover with a passion for wild places, I came to the site to relax, observe, photograph and write about anything that inspired me.

It was February 2018, and it transpired that I was about to experience what the staff on the site described as the coldest winter they had experienced for 50 years. I had only been on the site for three weeks when the pipes froze, then burst. I had no running water for five days, ran out of bottled water, and ended up melting snow to cook and wash with. For four days, I lost my two rescue cats, which had come to live with me, and which I had let outside after two weeks—they were desperate to go out and hated being locked up. They eventually returned, none the worse for wear, and have been with me ever since.

The whole site was frozen solid and virtually cut off, as six-foot snow drifts blocked the roads. When the thaw eventually came, serious damage had been done to many of the caravans.

I had only been on site a few weeks when the 'Beast from the East' struck. It certainly was a chastening experience when the heating failed temporarily and the temperature inside the caravan dropped to below zero. Indeed, I woke one morning to find the water in the cats' drinking bowls practically frozen solid, and extra layers of clothing and bedding—and thermal hats indoors—became a must.

I had my mountain bike with me, but cycling was impossible in the snow. I did manage to walk to a nearby shop in search of supplies: a walk of 45 minutes under the freezing conditions. I filled my rucksack with essentials, then returned to my caravan. The site manager and a skeleton staff did their best to bring in basic things like bread and milk, but even the manager's powerful Jeep could not reach the site every day, and the site office, which was usually open from 9 a.m. to 5 p.m., opened for just one hour a day.

When the snow did finally melt and things returned to some semblance of normality, I found myself with a bill for a few hundred pounds for the repair of frozen pipes and burst taps. But I had got off very lightly, as some caravan owners found their boilers had burst, and a few caravans were completely flooded, and carpets and furniture ruined.

When my mother came to visit, she casually remarked that, 'I had experienced trial, not by fire, but by ice!' It made me laugh, but in some ways she was right.

And, of course, at this juncture, unknown to me, I was yet to experience what I believe to be the hottest summer we had ever had in Great Britain. I was at Junior School, in Devizes in Wiltshire, during the long, hot, balmy summer of 1976, but surely the 2018 summer's extended heatwave was at least as hot, if not hotter?

Yes, I had certainly experienced trial by ice—trial by fire was yet to come!

The summer on the site was, of course, a complete contrast to the freezing conditions of winter. The 'Beast from the East' was now a distant memory, and as temperatures rose, then soared, I took every opportunity I had to explore, and seek out the wildlife and spectacular scenery the area had to offer.

With the coming of spring, the trees, once skeletal and devoid of foliage, began to flourish. Flowers, both wild and cultivated, blossomed beneath my caravan, and animals such as hedgehogs emerged from their winter sleep to forage for food.

As a member of Butterfly Conservation, I built my own moth trap, using an ultraviolet lamp and an old storage box. I trapped many moths in the trap, which I left out overnight on the decking of my caravan. Turning over the egg boxes and investigating what I had caught was a real pleasure, and, of course, I made sure all the moths were released unharmed the following night.

It was a good year for butterflies, and painted ladies, red admirals, peacocks, and the occasional small tortoiseshell visited the buddleia belonging to a neighbour. Indeed, I even managed to photograph a jersey tiger moth: a large and beautifully marked moth first discovered in Wales in 2008, on that very same buddleia. I reported this find to Butterfly Conservation, who were extremely interested in my sighting and assured me that the moths were now breeding on the Glamorganshire coastline.

With the improvement in the weather, I took every opportunity I had to explore the local nature reserve at Lavernock, look for fossils on the beach, and visit Cosmeston Country Park, which with its myriad habitats for wildlife is a magnet for all manner of bird life. Sully Island, steeped in history, is less than a quarter of a mile away, but crossing to the island across the causeway can be treacherous. It is especially important to be aware of tides, which can catch out the unwary and sweep in with surprising speed.

To be honest, the summer was a little too hot for me, and perhaps for a lot of other people as well. But as I walked and cycled much of the area, familiarising myself with my environment, I was able to watch birds such as buzzards, sparrowhawks and the occasional peregrine falcon hunting for prey.

The summer and the heat seemed to go on forever, but of course, with the onset of autumn, the temperatures finally dropped, and my world got colder once again.

It is nearly November now, still dark, and exceedingly early in the morning, and I can hear tawny owls calling from the woods as I put the finishing touches to this article and reflect on the year I have experienced. Yes, it is getting colder; but temperatures are not as cold as they were when I first arrived on the caravan site in February, when the 'Beast from the East' blew in and held the country in the grip of its icy tentacles.

I hope temperatures will not get that cold again.

On December 1st, I will move from the site to a holiday cottage I have rented on a working sheep farm near the hamlet of White Mill, in rural Carmarthenshire.

I intend to use this extended break to research and write a book.

My writing retreat is to be an extended holiday but, of course, with a difference.

Will the 'Beast from the East' come back to haunt me when I return to live in my caravan in February 2019?

I certainly hope not!

CARMARTHENSHIRE
A RURAL RETREAT IN CARMARTHENSHIRE

Pantgwyn Farm, and the cottage, which is on the left.

It was winter 2018 when I went to live for two months in a cottage on a working arable and sheep farm in rural Carmarthenshire, south-west Wales. I arrived on the first day of December and would stay until the beginning of February the following year. I hoped to use my extended break to research and write a series of articles, or possibly even a book, and venture as far afield as my mountain bike would carry me. I had no car, so I had to rely on my legs to get around, and it was inevitable that I'd become much fitter as I clocked up the miles.

The cottage, on Pantgwyn Farm, a mile from the hamlet of White Mill, was situated on an exceedingly steep hill and was quite isolated. The terrain and vistas of a Welsh hill farm were a complete contrast to the coastal landscape I had left behind in the Vale of Glamorgan, but the views across the valley were magnificent and an absolute delight for a nature lover like myself.

The town of Carmarthen was five miles away, and apart from a convenience store one mile from the farm, it was the nearest place to shop. This meant that every time I left the cottage to explore the area or simply stock up on provisions, I had to cycle up that hill. The road up the hill was a mile long and twisted and turned like a giant serpent as it snaked its way seemingly ever upwards. Over the months, I got to know that hill exceptionally well!

The cottage at Lower Mill Barn, set in the grounds of the owners' 17th-century farmhouse, was very cosy, compact and warm. I felt completely at home—even when the wind howled and the rain hammered against the outside of the building. The valley I viewed from my lounge window stretched for miles, with few signs of human habitation, to a lush, verdant horizon.

I had brought my two cats with me. They were rescue cats originally and were exceedingly nervous in their new surroundings. I did not let them leave the cottage for the first ten days, even though they constantly pestered me. Clearly, they did not like being 'incarcerated', and despite their nervousness, they were clearly desperate to explore their brand-new world on the farm.

The farm's owners kept a working sheepdog, a King Charles spaniel, a guinea fowl, a miniature Shetland pony and a cat. The pony, the cat and the guinea fowl lived permanently outdoors, but had shelter if they needed. The dogs lived in the farmhouse, but were often outside, whilst the few sheep they kept were more akin to pets than animals destined for market.

I was acutely aware that my cats would require a gentle introduction to this menagerie. I did not want my cats to be spooked, and I did not want them to spook the owner's animals. When I finally did let them out, they took to their new surroundings without a hitch, and there were no issues whatsoever with all the other creatures on the farm. My male cat, I Ching (that is the name he came with when I rescued him, and apparently, it is bad luck to change a cat's name), did growl at the miniature Shetland pony once, but the little pony took no offence and carried on eating.

For the first week, apart from cycling into Carmarthen several times and walking the hills around the farm, I stayed close to the cottage, in part, to make sure that my cats were settling in.

It rained regularly on the farm, but on a cold, crisp day when the winter sun lit up the valley, it was a joy to watch red kites soar in the azure skies, seemingly floating above the red deer which had gathered in the deer park across the far side of the valley. Buzzards were also a frequent sight, and together with the kites, these magnificent raptors would use the air currents to assist them as they climbed ever higher into the skies.

In the mornings, when I opened a window to let my cats outside, I would listen to the tinkling of a tiny stream which tumbled over a miniature waterfall only a few feet away from the cottage. A myriad of songbirds visited the bird table and feeding station in the farmhouse garden, and I marvelled at the melodious sounds of the dawn chorus, which awoke me daily from my slumber.

A View Across the Valley

At night, as darkness fell, the only lights visible for miles across the valley were those of an isolated farmhouse. When it was calm, sometimes all you could hear was the haunting cry of a tawny owl or the bleat of a solitary sheep and, of course, the tinkling of that tiny stream as it tumbled and tumbled down the hillside.

Between Christmas and New Year, I took the chance to venture further, this time taking a different route and direction. On one particular day, I cycled into Carmarthen, then followed the coastal path for a few miles in a southerly direction. The path ran alongside the River Towy in places, but I often found myself cycling along the road, then through woodland, where the paths were clogged with autumn leaves and mud, which sapped my strength as I slid about in the leaf-mould quagmire.

The coastal path was not well signposted, and although I always carried an Ordnance Survey map, in several places the blue arrows which marked the route had become detached and fallen to the ground. This made it difficult to follow the path itself. I cycled 18 miles that day, and by the time I returned to the cottage, both my bike and I were caked in cloying Carmarthenshire mud and leaves.

With New Year approaching, I bought a nice bottle of Welsh whisky to celebrate the turning of the year. My cat Chi-Chi celebrated her eleventh birthday on the 1st of January, and I toasted her and wished her and I Ching all the best for 2019, then wished all the inhabitants of the farm, both human and animal alike, a happy, healthy and prosperous year to come!

In the first week of January, I again ventured into Carmarthen. I was developing a real fondness for the county town. It was on my return, as I climbed the hill above White Mill to my cottage at Lower Mill Barn, that I witnessed up to 25 red kites wheeling and soaring in a flock above the fields. I had seen red kites before when travelling through the French and Spanish Pyrenees some years previously, but to see them in Britain—and in such numbers, when once they were virtually wiped out—was a real treat.

As I got halfway up the hill, I stopped to chat to a local landowner, who was only too eager to show me around his campsite, which catered for tourists in the warmer months. As we chatted, a friend of his, who was a builder, pulled up in a battered and distinctly dilapidated Ford Fiesta.

'Can you smell it? It smells like a chip shop,' the campsite's owner said.

'It runs on recycled vegetable oil!' his builder friend interjected and assured me that his car was as efficient as any petrol-driven vehicle on the road.

For a tired cyclist, the smell was overpowering, and I thought it a shame that at that moment, there was no way of deep-frying some chips in the fuel tank, as a large portion, wrapped in some old newspaper and sprinkled with salt and vinegar, would have done just the job!

The next few weeks were to prove rather eventful, and I continued to explore Carmarthen with its long and distinguished history. The gaol, which was once where the County Council buildings now stand, has a rather macabre past stretching back centuries. Little remains of the castle, but the gatehouse is still there.

I regularly cycled past the Roman amphitheatre and learned about the nearby fort, constructed when Carmarthen was a Roman settlement. Down by the river, I discovered some coracles neatly stacked and stored in a building. They looked perfectly 'river-worthy', and I guessed that they might be for sale or used frequently.

As I continued to explore, I would buy local produce, including speciality cheeses, from the indoor market and the small shops dotted around the town centre. Shops which, overall, used local ingredients whenever possible when preparing their own food for sale.

Back on the farm, I awoke one morning to find the farm's owner, Les, who was in his seventies, with his leg in plaster. Apparently, he had blacked out and fallen in the bathroom in the farmhouse. He had broken his leg, but the blackout, according to his wife, Karen, was not the first. In hospital, whilst having his broken leg repaired, it was also discovered that Les had heart problems, and he was to have a pacemaker fitted.

I felt deeply sorry for him, as for such a seemingly fit and active person, his life had changed forever. I told his wife Karen that if she ever needed any help on the farm with tasks, then she could ask me. I knew I was not able to drive a tractor! But, within reason, I was there to help. Karen thanked me and said she would call on me if the need arose.

The call, however, never came. I think Karen, who was quite a few years younger than Les, was proudly self-sufficient, and judging by the way she wielded a chainsaw and carried out many of the tasks on the farm, it was obvious she was more than competent.

There were so many little pleasures I took from my stay at the cottage.

A flock of sheep, perhaps 100 strong, would pass by my window, which overlooked a field at the rear of the cottage, daily. The sheep were no longer nervous of me, as they had been when I first arrived. And when I called to them, it was obvious they had become used to my presence, as they no longer ran away.

At certain times of the day, I would watch with regularity a murmuration of starlings in that same field, before they settled to feed on the insects and seeds in the grass. There were perhaps 500 birds in the flock, seemingly moving as one, swooping and rising like a single entity—a billowing blanket of birds which captivated and transfixed me with their sinuous movement each afternoon.

I often walked the deer park across the other side of the valley, marvelling at the size and majesty of the red deer stags which, separated from the hinds and fawns, gathered in small bachelor-herds in their small, enclosed fields.

On January 21st, in the early hours of the morning, I was treated to an incredibly special event: a total lunar eclipse combined with a blood moon. At about 4 a.m. that morning, with the skies clear and the stars twinkling in the heavens, I watched that blood-red moon, also known as a super blood wolf moon, change from red to black as the eclipse ran its course. For a few minutes the sky went completely dark, then the blood-red moon reappeared once more, accompanied by the twinkling of those tiny pinpoint stars, which once again flickered in the heavens. It was an astonishing event to witness, and one which will not re-occur for another 18 years.

On the 27th of January, a massive storm battered the farm and the valley. The wind raged and roared throughout the night, bringing down large trees and branches. In the morning, when the storm had abated, I helped clear the farmyard of debris, piling up sticks and branches. Under the circumstances, with Les incapacitated, I felt it was the least I could do. My time on Pantgwyn Farm was coming to an end. I had walked and cycled approximately 350 miles during my extended break in the Carmarthenshire hills. On the 1st of February, I took one last walk through the deer park, watching birds such as bramblings, redwings, kites—and of course, the always imposing red deer.

The following morning, I said goodbye to Les, Karen and their teenage son, Harvey, wishing Les all the best for his future and hoping he would make a full recovery from illness and injury. I then said my goodbyes to all the animals on the farm, leaving little Smokey, their 18-year-old cat, who I had developed a real fondness for, until last. Smokey seemed to sense that I was leaving and meowed constantly, rubbing herself against me as I fed her—something she had never done before.

In the clear, azure-blue skies above Pantgwyn Farm, the birds were gathering. The farmer had ploughed a field across the far side of the valley, and the kites, buzzards, crows and songbirds had descended en masse to feed on the insects and worms churned up by his plough. As I gazed into those bright blue skies, red kites and buzzards were also flocking in considerable numbers. I imagined the flapping of their huge wings as a kind of valediction. A waving goodbye, perhaps, to a dear old friend who was so grateful to visit their green and verdant valley. An old friend who would miss the delights of rural Carmarthenshire, but one who'd had a wonderful and uplifting experience. An experience which would remain with him for the rest of his life.

THE NATIONAL BOTANIC GARDENS OF WALES

The Gardens in Summer. Image copyright Tim Jones Photography

A summer visit to the National Botanic Gardens of Wales, when birdsong and the buzzing of busy insects fills the air, is a must for anyone keen on the wonders of nature. Set in the stunning Carmarthenshire countryside, the garden was opened in May 2000 and has since been visited by more than 2.5 million people. Plaudits received include the Gold Accolade by Visit Wales and being voted 'number 1 garden to visit in the principality' by viewers of BBC *Gardeners' World*. Visitors will find a comprehensive collection of over 8,000 plant varieties set in a landscape of 560 acres.

The Gardens in Summer. Image copyright Tim Jones Photography

The garden, with its mission to conserve, educate and inspire, as a charity funded by the Welsh Government and Carmarthenshire County Council, aims to nurture diversity and sustainability. It is open daily throughout the year except Christmas Eve and Christmas Day, with entry free for carers and under-fives. If you cycle and show your helmet, the admission fee is halved—a concession for using a greener form of transport. For car drivers, minibuses and coach parties, there is plenty of parking space.

There is so much to see there that you will need a full day. Amongst the attractions is the 200-year-old Double Walled Garden, where the stone outer and brick interior walls create a series of different microclimates; it is thought that this was to extend the growing season. Today, the garden is split into four quadrants. Three tell the story of flowering plants, from primitive water lilies to the latest cultivars, while the fourth is a modern kitchen garden where vegetables are grown which you will find on your plate in the Botanic Garden's Seasons Restaurant in the Stable Block.

The Great Glasshouse

The Apothecary's Garden is full of healing herbs, and next door lies the Apothecary's Hall. This Edwardian pharmacy is packed full of medicinal memorabilia from books to bottles and jars of tinctures, syrups and powders. There is also the Bee Garden, home to 250,000 honeybees, where the hives have large viewing windows, and the Wild Garden, which shimmers with sweeping colours throughout the summer. At the Bird of Prey Centre you can watch displays of raptors such as owls, kites, falcons, buzzards and even golden eagles, and if you wish, you can even fly certain birds yourself.

The garden is also a great place to learn, with an organic working farm, a National Nature Reserve, and Principality House. This regency building hosts conferences, seminars and training days. There are curriculum-linked programmes for schools and colleges, facilitated by a friendly team.

Even on rainy days, there is so much to see, including the Great Glasshouse, the largest single-span glasshouse on the planet, with the largest collection of Mediterranean plants in the Northern Hemisphere. My reaction as I moved inside was simply 'Wow!' The interior surpassed all my expectations, with flowers, trees and shrubs from across the world growing in abundance in miniature replicas of landscapes you would find in countries such as Australia, South Africa and Chile—and all under one enormous glass roof. Footpaths wind their way around and between these micro-environments, so viewing is accessible and easy for young and old alike.

After meandering around for some considerable time, marvelling at those miniature landscapes—some of which had a passing resemblance to the film set of *Jurassic Park* (though, of course, without the dinosaurs)—I left the Great Glasshouse and headed for the Ghost Forest. This display of tropical tree roots from Ghana is one of the most significant environmental art installations to come to Wales. The oldest tree root is 300 years old; the heaviest weighs 19 tonnes. The work is the creation of artist Angela Palmer. Horrified to learn that tropical forest the size of a rugby pitch is destroyed every four seconds, she wanted to make ambassadors out of the uprooted trees as a reminder to protect the environment. She chose Ghana as it now sustainably manages its rainforests.

As a proud member of Butterfly Conservation, I could not wait to visit the Tropical Butterfly House, and once inside, I was not disappointed. Magnificent, iridescent, blue morpho butterflies, some as large as my hand, flitted amongst foliage which resembled a miniature jungle. Other garish butterflies sipped sugars from segments of soft fruits such as melon and peach. At one point, a magnificent blue morpho butterfly settled on the stomach of a young woman who was wearing a white dress—apparently butterflies are attracted to the colour white. Her partner then explained that his girlfriend was pregnant, so this seemed a particularly touching moment

Butterflies Nectaring on Fruit, The Tropical Butterfly House

as the butterfly remained on her dress for some time, flashing its shimmering, jewel-like wings as it posed and postured for his camera.

If it is a dull day outside, many of the butterflies will gather at the windows for the extra warmth they might obtain through the glass. Heat is especially important to butterflies, as they need to warm up to fuel their flight muscles and stay active.

A member of staff was on a placement from Butterfly Conservation, and she seemed deeply knowledgeable about her subject matter. She was gluing—yes, gluing—several different pupae to a wooden board. When a caterpillar metamorphoses into a pupae or chrysalis, it secretes a sticky substance from one end to attach itself to a leaf, tree or branch and hangs until the adult butterfly emerges. The glue would do the pupae no harm and was only replicating what would occur in nature.

Many of the garden's specimens were bought from butterfly farms around the country and sometimes they also purchased moths, including the giant atlas moth—the world's largest moth, with a wingspan of nearly a foot. I did not see an atlas moth that day, but it did not really matter, as I was just enthralled to be in the company of such stunning and majestic insects. Insects which I had carefully nurtured and maintained a fascination for since I was young.

It was with great reluctance that I finally left the Tropical Butterfly House and the National Botanic Garden of Wales. I promised myself I would return to experience the garden again, as I was so taken with the scents and stunning colours of my surroundings, which resonated with the sounds of birdsong and the incessant humming of busy insects—creatures which are so vital to the health of the garden and the planet on which we live.

A planet which we neglect at our peril.

POSTSCRIPT

Very sadly, since the time of my visit to the National Botanic Gardens of Wales, there are no longer butterflies or moths in the Tropical House. Unfortunately, they fell victim to Covid regulations. At the time of writing this book, it is not known whether they will ever return.

Author Profile

Marc Harris was born in Cardiff in 1962. Marc has previously written three books. Two of these were Rhythms of Nature, a poetry book, and Sentience, a poetry pamphlet. A third book, Wild Tales & Rural Rides, an anthology of travel and nature writing, containing non-fiction, poems and short stories, was published in 2018.

Marc has also written articles and short stories for many magazines, including Evergreen, Explore England, This England and The Countryman, and specialist fishing magazines such as Fallon's Angler and Waterlog.

An accomplished poet, Marc's poems have been published in high-profile magazines such as Agenda, Poetry Ireland and The New Welsh Review.

He now divides his time between a house in Dinas Powys, where he lives for part of the year, and a caravan with stunning views of the sea, overlooking the islands of Flat Holm and Steep Holm in the Vale of Glamorgan.

He lives with his two rescue cats, which keep him company and entertained, and which he adores.

What Did You Think of *South and West Wales: Its Wildlife, People and Places?*

A big thank you for purchasing this book. It means a lot that you chose this book specifically from such a wide range on offer. I do hope you enjoyed it.

Book reviews are incredibly important for an author. All feedback helps them improve their writing for future projects and for developing this edition. If you are able to spare a few minutes to post a review on Amazon, that would be much appreciated.

Publisher Information

Rowanvale Books provides publishing services to independent authors, writers and poets all over the globe. We deliver a personal, honest and efficient service that allows authors to see their work published, while remaining in control of the process and retaining their creativity. By making publishing services available to authors in a cost-effective and ethical way, we at Rowanvale Books hope to ensure that the local, national and international community benefits from a steady stream of good quality literature.

For more information about us, our authors or our publications, please get in touch.

www.rowanvalebooks.com
info@rowanvalebooks.com

Printed in Great Britain
by Amazon